I'm dedicating this children's book to my wonderful daughter, McKenzie. You are my heart, my treasure, and the reason I strive to be a better woman every day. Thank you for being you.

A T.S. Connor Book
Published by T.S. Connor

ISBN: 978-1-5136-8619-6

McKenzie

&

Michael

a T.S. Connor Book
Illustrated by Travis A. Thompson

While McKenzie lies
in her bed

She silently cries, and
tears she sheds

She holds her teddy
bear really tight

And prays it protects
her with all her might

She wipes her eyes with vision cleared

When all of a sudden a glowing figure appears

I know the fussing and fighting makes you scared

But always remember, when it comes to you, your parents truly care

You may not understand now, but soon you'll discover

Your parents really love you and each other

I know things have been crazy with daddy and I

But I need you to know there's no need to cry

You've been so patient with us, and you're the best kid in the world

Even when daddy and I disagree, you'll always be my favorite little girl

I know you miss the love that daddy and I have once shown

Which is why I'm happy to tell you that daddy and I are working things out, and he's coming back home

Did you hear that?!
I can't wait for him to
meet you! He'll be so glad
that you came!

I have to tell him about
my new friend!
What is your name?

My name is Michael, but only you can see me

I know your parents had some problems before, but everything's working out how they should be

Divine timing and fate makes sure everything works out in the end

And if you need me just call on me

I will always be your protective friend

Author T.S. Connor

She's a poet, spoken word artist, and fiction novelist who love all things creative. She was introduced to writing poetry at nine-years-old, and have been in love with the power of words ever since. Now, as a mother, soon to be wife, and self-made entrepreneur, she hopes to inspire other creative souls to shine their God given creative light in a too often dim world. In essence, she aspires to pass down the creative torch to future generations.

CPSIA information can be obtained
at www.ICGtesting.com
Printed in the USA
LVHW061040020721
691051LV00024B/1602